The legend of *Robin Hood* has been passed down the centuries, through folklore, ballads and plays. *Robin Hood* became a particularly popular figure in 19th century literature, and his adventures continue to captivate people today.

© 1993 Twin Books Ltd

Produced by
TWIN BOOKS LTD
Kimbolton House
117A Fulham Road
London SW3 6RL
England

Directed by CND – Muriel Nathan-Deiller
Illustrated by Van Gool-Lefèvre-Loiseaux
Text adapted by Sue Jackson

ISBN: 1 85469 928 8

Printed in Hong Kong

This edition printed 1994

Robin Hood

TWIN BOOKS

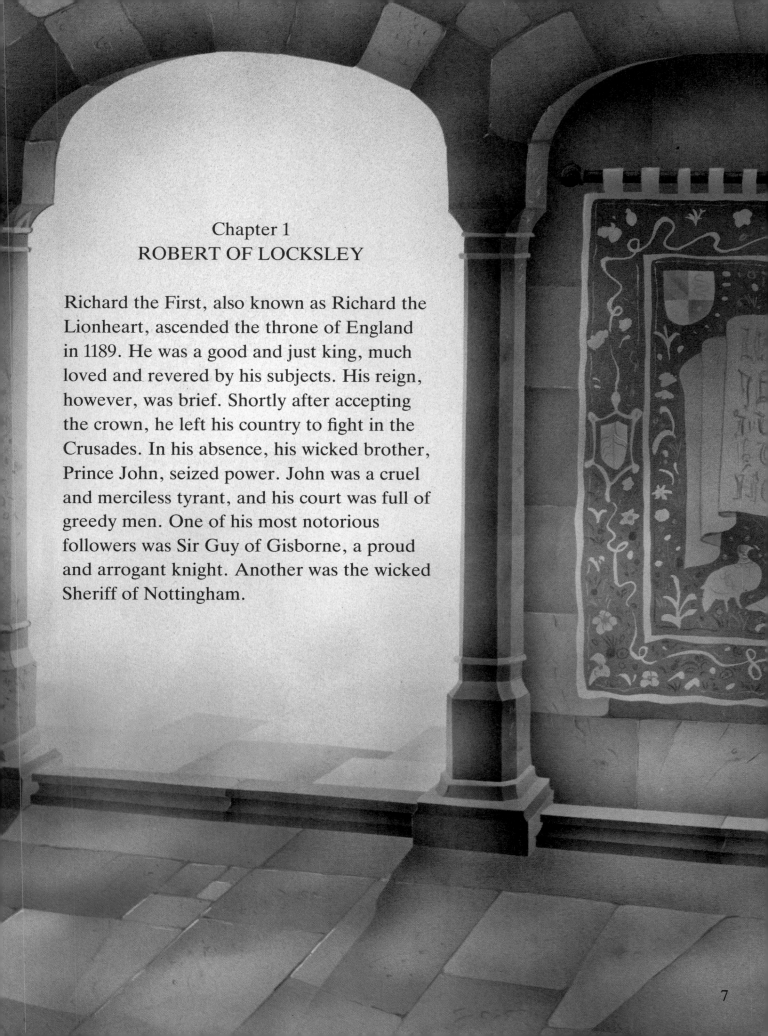

Chapter 1
ROBERT OF LOCKSLEY

Richard the First, also known as Richard the Lionheart, ascended the throne of England in 1189. He was a good and just king, much loved and revered by his subjects. His reign, however, was brief. Shortly after accepting the crown, he left his country to fight in the Crusades. In his absence, his wicked brother, Prince John, seized power. John was a cruel and merciless tyrant, and his court was full of greedy men. One of his most notorious followers was Sir Guy of Gisborne, a proud and arrogant knight. Another was the wicked Sheriff of Nottingham.

One fine day, Prince John, the Sheriff of Nottingham, and several members of the court were hunting deer in Sherwood Forest, when, in a clearing, they stumbled upon a peasant skinning a deer.

"Seize that man!" cried Prince John. "The forest laws forbid anyone, except members of the Royal Court, to hunt and kill deer. The penalty for your crime, peasant, is death!"

"Have pity, sire!" gasped the serf. "My children are hungry."

"If you want to live," answered Prince John, "tell me where I can find Robin Hood."

Robin Hood, according to the Sheriff of Nottingham, was a local outlaw, loyal to King Richard, who spent his days robbing the rich to help the poor.

The serf was speechless. What choice did he have? Should he suffer death, and abandon his family? Could he betray Robin? Finally, he mumbled, "Seek him at Locksley Castle."

"Beware if you lie!" warned the sheriff in parting. "For I shall return to punish you."

The following day, Prince John, accompanied by Guy of Gisborne and their men-at-arms, went to Locksley Castle. In the Grand Hall, they saw a young knight – Robert of Locksley – addressing a large crowd. A banquet was being held to celebrate his betrothal to Lady Marian, the beautiful and fearless daughter of Lord Fitzwalter.

"If Robert of Locksley is Robin Hood, we should prevent him from marrying such a noble and beautiful woman," declared Guy of Gisborne. He had other plans for Maid Marian!

"To listen to him speak," commented Prince John, "you would think that Sherwood Forest was his, and its inhabitants Robert of Lockley's personal army preparing for war."

Noticing their presence, Robert of Locksley broke off his speech, and called out, "Beware, my friends! The usurper, Prince John, and his followers are in our midst."

Chapter 2
SHERWOOD FOREST

Panic broke out in the banqueting hall. At Prince John's command, his men advanced towards Robin Hood, for indeed Robert of Locksley was none other than the outlaw! Robin's followers drew their swords, and attacked the intruders. Tables were overturned and the guests dispersed, as the hall became a battleground. In the confusion, Robin escaped, closely followed by his men.

Finally order was restored. "From this day forth, Robert of Locksley forfeits all his lands and titles," decreed Prince John. "Any news leading to the capture of this infamous outlaw will be well rewarded!"

Proud as a peacock. Gisborne strutted towards Lady Marian. He had decided that she was to be his wife! But before he could reach her side, Marian stood up and bravely announced to the remaining guests, "I will remain forever loyal to Robert of Locksley."

Robin, with his followers, established his camp in a large, dry cave at the heart of Sherwood Forest. He lacked only two things – money and the company of Maid Marian.

"My friends, we are in desperate need of funds if we are to live in the forest and defend ourselves against Prince John's men," he said to his companions, a few days later. "Is there anyone among you who will risk his life to retrieve the gold hidden at Locksley Castle?"

Each and every man volunteered.

"Thank you, one and all," responded Robin, greatly moved by their loyalty. "I would like to suggest Will Scarlet and Little John for this mission. Prince John has never met Will, and Little John, blindfolded, knows his way around the forest. Good luck, my friends! Return safely."

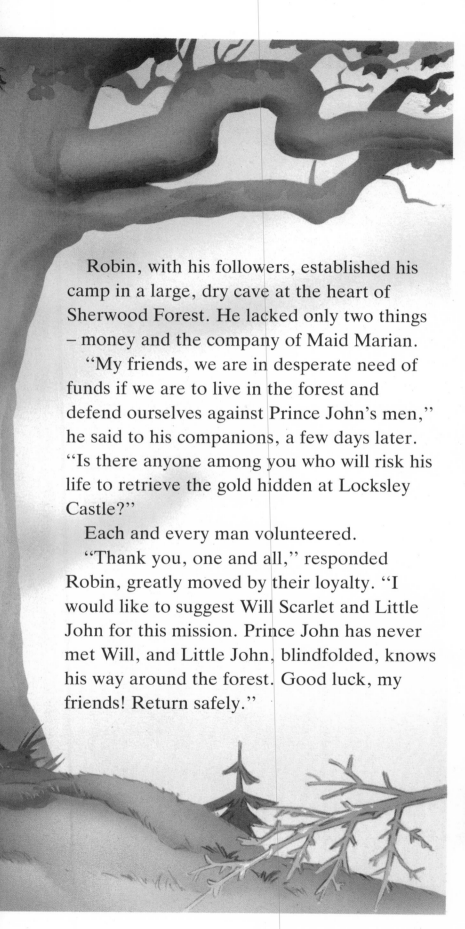

Will Scarlet and Little John cautiously approached Locksley Castle. Hidden from view at the edge of the forest, they watched Guy of Gisborne and Maid Marian walking in the castle grounds.

"Lady Marian, Robin Hood has deserted you! I, therefore, humbly offer you my love and my allegiance. Be mine!" pleaded Sir Guy.

"Good sire", replied Maid Marian politely, "I thank you for your kind offer. But my heart belongs to Robin. I will wait for him."

"Do you hear that, Will?" asked Little John. "Now go to the castle, and gain entry through the kitchen. Robin hid the gold in two sacks in the cellar. I will wait for you here."

Little John waited until evening. There was no sign of Will. Had he been captured?

A furtive shadow crept along the castle wall.

"Are you still there?" called Will anxiously. Little John crept towards him.

"I have the gold. Let's go quickly, before the soldiers are alerted to my escape," whispered Will.

Will and Little John returned to the hideaway in the forest, totally exhausted.

"The Sheriff of Nottingham was going to have me thrown into the dungeons, when Friar Tuck came to my rescue," Will told his companions.

"Who's Friar Tuck?" asked Robin.

"He's a monk, and a loyal supporter of King Richard. I have asked him to sup with us tonight," replied Will.

Friar Tuck, that evening, ate enough for three, and drank his fill before delivering his news. "The king, returning home from the Crusades, was captured in Austria," he reported, "and the Austrians are now demanding a large ransom for his release. Prince John, of course, wishes his brother dead and therefore will not help. It falls to us to raise the ransom monies if the king is ever to regain his throne."

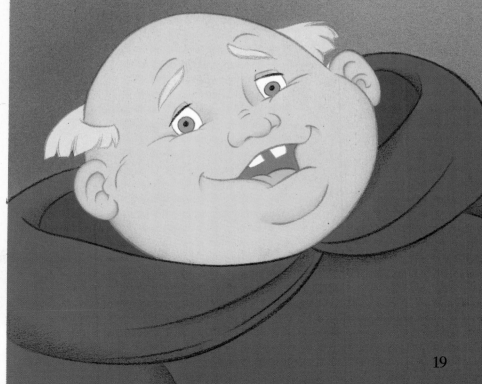

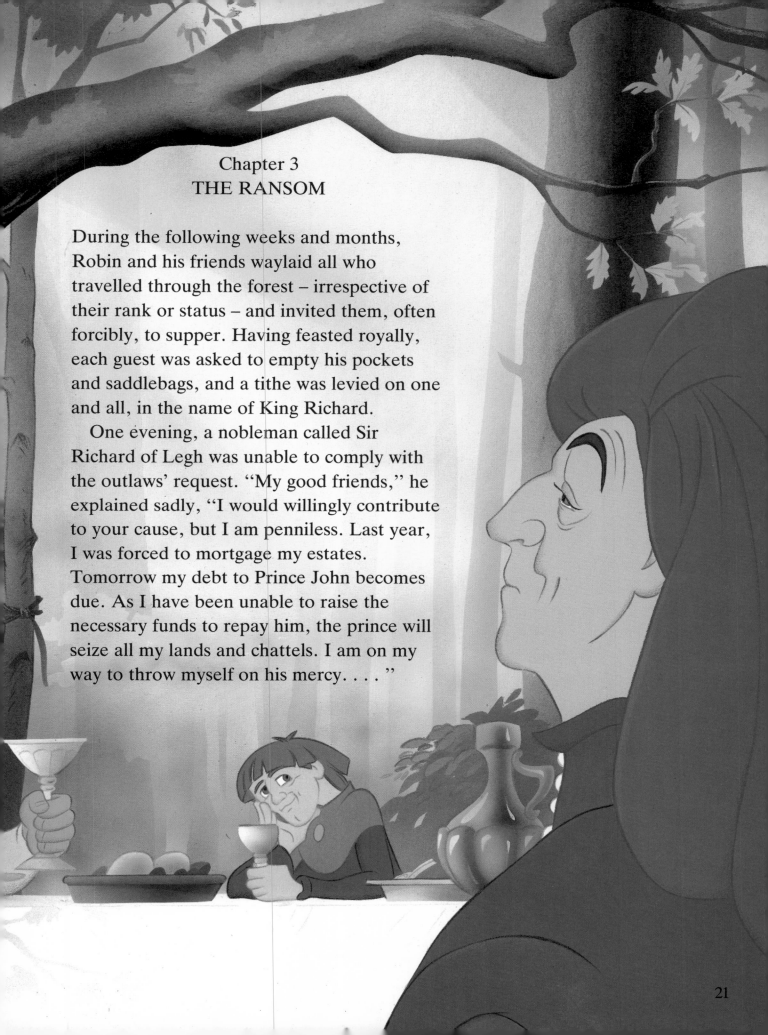

Chapter 3
THE RANSOM

During the following weeks and months, Robin and his friends waylaid all who travelled through the forest – irrespective of their rank or status – and invited them, often forcibly, to supper. Having feasted royally, each guest was asked to empty his pockets and saddlebags, and a tithe was levied on one and all, in the name of King Richard.

One evening, a nobleman called Sir Richard of Legh was unable to comply with the outlaws' request. "My good friends," he explained sadly, "I would willingly contribute to your cause, but I am penniless. Last year, I was forced to mortgage my estates. Tomorrow my debt to Prince John becomes due. As I have been unable to raise the necessary funds to repay him, the prince will seize all my lands and chattels. I am on my way to throw myself on his mercy. . . ."

The following day, as the sun rose, Sir Richard presented himself at Locksley Castle, where Prince John was holding court. The prince was in an excellent mood. Today his estates were to be substantially enlarged!

Sir Richard approached the dais. "Prince John, I have come to repay the debt on my lands," he announced proudly.

Prince John raged. Where had Sir Richard found the money in so short a time? Had he stolen it?

Sir Richard offered no explanation. He had found a new friend in Robin Hood! The outlaw had lent Sir Richard the gold, and between them they had foiled another of Prince John's plans!

Meanwhile, in his castle, Lord Fitzwalter pleaded with his daughter, "My dear child, not a day goes by without Sir Guy asking me for your hand in marriage. What am I to do?"

"There is only one answer, Father," replied Maid Marian patiently.

"I am afraid," replied her father. "If you won't marry Sir Guy, he will think I am a loyal supporter of King Richard, and therefore a sworn enemy of Prince John. The prince has a fearsome temper and will undoubtedly seek revenge."

Marian considered the issue. "Father," she proposed, "when Sir Guy next visits, summon me to your presence. The castle will have to be searched from top to bottom, for I shall not be here. I shall leave, without warning, then neither the prince nor Sir Guy will be able to hold you responsible for my obstinate refusal."

Sir Guy returned to see Lord Fitzwalter the following day.

"I have waited far too long for an answer!" he shouted impatiently. "You must insist that Lady Marian marries me!"

"Certainly, sire" replied the old man, trembling. "Marian is stubborn. . . ." He called to a servant, "Ask my daughter to join us."

Lord Fitzwalter led Sir Guy to dinner. The knight consumed two flasks of wine, and devoured several roast fowl before the servant returned, out of breath.

"Excuse me, my Lord, but Lady Marian is nowhere to be found. Her maid said she awoke early this morning, but she has not been seen since," he gasped.

Sir Guy exploded with rage!

Robin was tracking deer in the forest when he spied a young unknown archer ambling along.

"Stand Sir, and explain your presence!" he challenged. No sooner had he spoken than the archer drew his bow and an arrow sped through the air, lifting off Robin's cap.

"Who do you think you are?" demanded Robin furiously.

"My lord, you *are* in a bad temper, today," laughed the archer, shaking his head in amusement. His hood fell off, and long blond tresses escaped down the archer's back.

"Marian! You have come to join us at last! Welcome," cried Robin Hood happily.

"I could wait no longer," declared Marian. "I have come to fight by your side until King Richard returns. From this day forth we shall never be parted!"

Months passed. Skirmishes with the Sheriff of Nottingham's men-at-arms, on patrol in the forest, became frequent occurrences. Robin and his followers were joined by many others, who were also seeking justice and the return of King Richard. Robin ensured that all were well fed and drilled in the art of warfare. Passing travellers were always encouraged – often on pain of death – to fill the outlaws' coffers!

One day, Sir Richard of Legh returned to the forest. "The harvest has been good this year," he announced joyfully, "and I am happy to repay, in full and with a hundred-fold interest, the sum you lent me a year ago today."

Robin was delighted. At last they had sufficient gold for King Richard's ransom! Sir Legh proudly left for Austria to bring the king home.

Chapter 4
AN EXECUTION

After Sir Richard's departure, life in the forest was quiet. Everyone keenly awaited King Richard's return, with little thought for the Sheriff of Nottingham or proud Guy of Gisborne. But the peace was soon broken!

One day, Robin and Marian were enjoying a walk together in the woods when they heard anguished cries. Will Scarlett ran towards them. Today, he certainly merited his name, for his face was bright red with exertion. He was also out of breath. "Little John has . . . The sheriff's men . . . have taken him. . . ." he gasped.

"What! Is he in prison?" asked Marian.

"And soon to be hanged!" replied Will.

"Fetch my arrows! To arms, my friends! We must rescue Little John!" rallied Robin.

Nottingham town square was bustling with activity. At the sheriff's command, gallows had been erected so that all could see the forthcoming execution. A cry went up for the hangman, who had not yet arrived.

A monk, the hood of his habit well drawn over his head, crossed the square, and approached the scaffold. "I have come to hear the prisoner's last confession," he said humbly to the soldiers, and continued on his way unchallenged.

Little John was escorted to the gallows. The monk, now standing at his side, spoke gently and quietly as if to comfort him.

"Little John, it's me – Robin," murmured the monk. "I have a knife up my sleeve with which to cut your bonds. Get ready to run when I give you the signal!"

Little John had great difficulty suppressing a smile of triumph!

Prince John, Guy of Gisborne and the Sheriff of Nottingham rode into the square. They examined the gallows closely, and nodded in approval.

"Sheriff, my compliments! You have, at last, managed to capture one of the outlaws. This public hanging will be an example to all, far and wide," said Prince John smugly.

The sheriff blushed with pride. But at that very moment, from all four corners of the square, rained down a shower of arrows. In the confusion, the prisoner broke free from his captors. Robin threw back his monk's hood, and drew out, from under the homespun habit, his bow and arrows. "Forward, my friends!" he cried. "For England and King Richard!"

Robin and his followers had the advantage of surprise, and were able to escape quickly through the crowd. The sheriff's soldiers, however – anticipating a large reward for the capture and execution of Little John – were furious at being cheated of their prize, and pursued Robin and his friends to the edge of the forest.

Robin and his men stood firm, and fought like lions. But they were outnumbered, and slowly lost ground as they tired.

Chapter 5
THE BLACK KNIGHT

Robin was about to give his men the signal to retreat, when a knight, dressed completely in black, rode to his side. Without a word, the knight drew his sword and launched into the fray. His appearance and his strength in battle not only amazed the sheriff's men, but also inspired Robin's followers to recommence battle with renewed energy. The fighting was fierce, and the soldiers soon fled.

"Hurrah!" cried Robin. "Once again the sheriff's men have been beaten." He turned to face the Black Knight. "We owe you our thanks, Sire. May I introduce my companions, all loyal subjects of King Richard. Those vanquished soldiers are in the service of the usurper, Prince John."

The Black Knight did not speak. He only bowed his head in acknowledgment, and then slowly rode away.

"Once again, you have failed!" screamed Prince John bitterly. "Robin Hood and his band of men now have a champion. Who is the Black Knight? Could he be an envoy from Richard, sent to overthrow me?"

"The only way to find out," suggested the sheriff, "is to entice him to declare himself!"

Prince John reflected for a moment. "Arrange a tournament in Nottingham, and invite all the knights and archers of the county," he instructed. "Neither the Black Knight nor Robin Hood will be able to resist the temptation to compete at such an event."

The Sheriff of Nottingham, bristling in anticipation, congratulated the prince on his ingenious plan.

Prince John was right! On the day of the tournament contestants swarmed into Nottingham.

Guy of Gisborne boasted that he would win the jousting tournament. As his reward, he was going to ask Prince John to grant him the hand of Maid Marian. His love and ambition made him fearless. He won joust after joust.

"Call my final adversary," cried Sir Guy enthusiastically. "All other competitors have ceded victory."

No sooner had he spoken than the Black Knight appeared at the far end of the field. His visor down and his lance poised, he charged. With apparently little effort, the Black Knight unseated Guy of Gisborne. The fallen knight found himself sitting, uninjured, on the ground beside his horse!

A hush fell over the crowd. Shame and disgrace had befallen Sir Guy! The Black Knight had won the tournament, without spilling a drop of blood!

"Black Knight," called Prince John, hardly disguising his anger, "You have won the tournament, without regard for the rules of chivalry. Nevertheless, approach! I would like to know your name so that I may congratulate you on your victory".

"Thank you for the compliment, Your Majesty," replied the Black Knight. "Regrettably, I cannot tarry. But, we'll meet again shortly!" And without further ado, he galloped away from the arena. Prince John was furious, and fearful! What was the Black Knight's quest?

Chapter 6
THE SILVER ARROW

The games continued. The archery competition commenced, but where was Robin? Surely he would compete. His skill with the bow and arrow was legendary.

The preliminary rounds were soon over. The contest lay between a nobleman representing the Forest of Barisdale – Prince John's champion – and a tall man dressed like a beggar.

"Prince John," wheezed Sir Guy. "The beggar must be Robin Hood. Have him arrested at once!"

"Sir Guy, that would be unwise," said the prince. "Robin's friends and supporters are here in force. Let him compete, we'll seize him later!"

The noble from Barisdale shot his arrow first. It went true to the target's bull's-eye.

The beggar drew his bow slowly, glanced at the distant target and then let his arrow fly. It sliced the nobleman's arrow in two. The crowd clapped and cheered.

"I declare this man to be the champion of archers," announced Prince John. "Throw off your hood, sir, so we may know who you are. Approach, and collect your prize – the symbol of your victory – the silver arrow."

"I am Robert of Locksley, also known as Robin Hood," the archer proudly declared, as he mounted the dais. The crowd gasped!

Prince John was powerless to act. If he were to arrest Robin now, the rules of chivalry would be infringed, and the crowd would riot.

"Outlaw, we meet at last!" he hissed. "Fear not. I *will* have my revenge!"

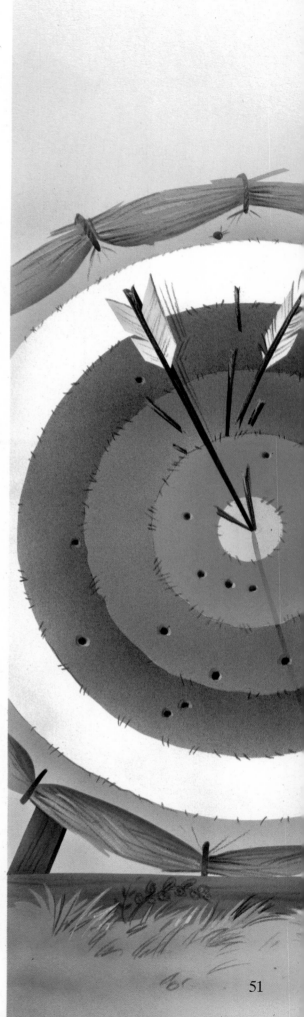

Robin left the tournament unhindered, followed by Maid Marian and his friends. To celebrate his victory, a banquet was arranged for that evening in Sherwood Forest.

While out hunting for a wild boar for the feast, Robin met the Black Knight. "Sire, beware!" Robin warned. "Prince John will have his revenge. Tomorrow his men-at-arms will scour the forest! Join us so that we may offer you our protection, as well as our loyalty and gratitude."

"Thank you for your invitation," replied the Black Knight courteously. "I would be pleased to accept you offer, but unfortunately my presence is required elsewhere. Perhaps I might join you later?"

"In that case," offered Robin, "take my horn. Should you be trapped by Prince John's soldiers while traversing the forest, blow once and I will come to your rescue."

"I shall not forget your loyalty," declared the Black Knight as he left.

53

Chapter 7
THE HORN

The following day, not long after dawn, the Black Knight was travelling through the forest when he found himself surrounded by a troop of the sheriff's men. He drew his sword and fought bravely. Escape was impossible! Before he was captured, he raised Robin's horn to his lips, and desperately blew one long rallying call.

"The Black Knight is in trouble," exclaimed Robin. "To arms, my friends! We must make haste to reach him. Marian join us! I fear that we will need all our strength and skill this time, to defeat the prince's forces."

Robin and his friends ran to the Black Knight's rescue. A fierce and bloody battle ensued, and many men fell on both sides. Finally, exhausted, and their numbers greatly depleted, the sheriff and his men turned and fled. Prince John and Sir Guy alone remained in the clearing, trapped by Robin's men.

Guy of Gisborne and Robin glared at each other for a long moment.

"We meet face to face at last!" exclaimed Robin. "You, Sir Guy, have pestered Lady Marian and her family for far too long. The time has come for us to settle our differences."

"Traitor!" shouted Sir Guy. "It will give me great pleasure to put you to death." He swiftly dismounted, and drew his sword.

Robin and Sir Guy fought long and hard, for they were evenly matched in both strength and skill. Finally, Sir Guy, exhausted, dropped his guard for an instant, and Robin seized the advantage. Sir Guy was no more!

Not a word had been spoken during the long duel; all eyes had been fixed on the contenders.

Robin, his victory assured, staggered to his feet. His friends sent up a loud cheer.

"Your loyalty and courage are known throughout the land, and today, I have witnessed both," declared the Black Knight, lifting off his helmet. "I, Richard the Lionheart, would now like to thank you, in person, for your support."

An astounded silence fell on the forest! Prince John gasped in terror! Richard turned to his brother. "Despite your treachery, John, I will spare your life, but you must leave England, with your entire court."

Robin knelt in front of his king, and signalled Marian to do the same. She threw off her cap, and her blond hair streamed down her back. King Richard smiled in amusement.

"For a woman," he commented, "you make an excellent soldier in battle, Madam. How can I repay your loyal service?"

"We have long awaited your return," replied Maid Marian, "and would now ask for your blessing on our marriage."

King Richard gave it willingly. He also restored all Robin's lands and titles. Robert of Locksley – accompanied by his wife – returned to his castle, nevermore to haunt the forest of Sherwood.

All England rejoiced when King Richard, once again, sat on the throne.